THIS BOOK
BELONGS TO

_____

PROVERBS
OF DON QUIXOTE

Greed always bursts the bag.

By the thread one comes to the ball of yarn.

Something is better than nothing at all.

Singing frightens away sorrows.

Man goes as God pleases.

To do good to fools is to pour water in the sea.

Fortune's wheel turns faster than a mill.

That which costs little is valued less.

A diamond is not as valuable as one's own tooth.

Tales of
DON
QUIXOTE

Tales of
DON
QUIXOTE
and His Friends

As Retold and Illustrated by

ONY PALAZZO

City Books · Garden City, N. Y.

This is a story of Don Quixote—
a man who loved a life of
adventure—

and this is his friend Sancho.
He helped Don in many ways
as you shall see.

This is an ordinary windmill—
but to Don it looked like a giant
with huge arms.

Then, here is Don's horse, Rosinante, and Sancho's donkey, Dapple.

They all became loyal companions and shared in many adventures, some gay and some sad.

CONTENTS

DON QUIXOTE BECOMES A KNIGHT

DON QUIXOTE had read of all the good deeds of knights of old; "I will become a knight, too," he decided. "I will exchange right for wrong, and laughter for tears, and happiness for unhappiness! Even as the knights of old, thought Don, I will travel and have many adventures!"

The first thing Don required as a knight was a suit of armor. He found the pieces in his attic that very afternoon.

Don polishes his grandfather's armor

They had belonged to his grandfather and were old and rusty. However, Don worked hard for three days and soon had a complete suit of armor that would make any knight proud.

*An ordinary horse...
better than any ordinary horse

AND CALLS HIM ROSINANTE *

"Now," thought Don, "I must find a horse that will help in my travels." He didn't have

to look far, for in his very own barn he found the very horse. He looked to be an ordinary horse. His bones stuck out like the corners of a tent and his back was shaped like a hammock. "I will call him Rosinante," exclaimed Don Quixote.

Don Quixote made himself ready as a grand knight of olden times.

There came the day when Rosinante was primped and the armor was polished and Don said good-bys. He traveled the high road leading from his village.

He looks at himself. fully dressed as a knight

SANCHO BECOMES DON QUIXOTE'S FRIEND

THE FIRST PERSON he met was a neighboring farmer called Sancho Panza. Don Quixote explained that he was on his way to seek adventure and right the wrongs of the world. Sancho begged to come along.

"Delighted," agreed Don.

"You shall be my assistant—and henceforward we shall work together!"

Sancho was delighted too and they traveled off down the road. Don Quixote, in full armor, sat astride Rosinante and Sancho rode his donkey, Dapple.

Don and Sancho
start on their adventures

THE ADVENTURE
OF THE WINDMILLS

THEY were barely out of the village when they spied some windmills.

"See," said Don Quixote, "ahead of us are thirty or forty giants each with four long arms."

"Giants? I see no giants, only windmills," replied the puzzled Sancho.

"It's easy to see you know nothing of adventure. Stand aside while I, Don Quixote, give them battle."

So saying, he spurred Rosinante on and charged!

Don gets stuck on the Windmill

As he reached the first windmill, the sails began to turn and caught Don's lance. He was lifted high into the air and Rosinante was flung into the next field. Poor Sancho was most unhappy. "Anyone could see they were nothing but windmills—I warned you, master!"

But Don Quixote was aching all over and did not reply immediately. As he mounted Rosinante—who was also aching all over—he spoke to Sancho.

"Fortune's wheel turns faster than a windmill and we will soon return and conquer those giants. Now let us continue on our way."

ROSINANTE WANTS
TO PLAY WITH STRANGERS

AFTER their adventure with the windmills Don Quixote and Sancho were weary and hungry. So were Rosinante and Sancho's Dapple. They found a shady, restful spot under a tree and Sancho opened the lunch box.

After unsaddling the horse and donkey Don and Sancho sat down to a quiet lunch and siesta.

*Don and Sancho
rest and have lunch*

The animals were not tied and they roamed the fields as they munched grass. Close by was a group of strange horses feeding.

Rosinante and Dapple
have lunch, too

Rosinante sees a group of strange horses

Rosinante, being a friendly horse, whinnied
long and loud, and wanted to romp and
make friends.

But, when they spied Rosinante running toward them, they became excited and unfriendly. They set upon him and kicked him! Even their owners could not quiet them!

The other horses
are unfriendly

All the rumpus awakened Don Quixote
and Sancho who ran to Rosinante's rescue.
When they left, Don Quixote, in a manner
unbecoming to a knight, had to ride
Sancho's donkey. Rosinante was too hurt
and was being led by faithful Sancho, on foot.

Rosinante is tired after his adventure so Don must ride Dapple

THE ADVENTURE OF THE

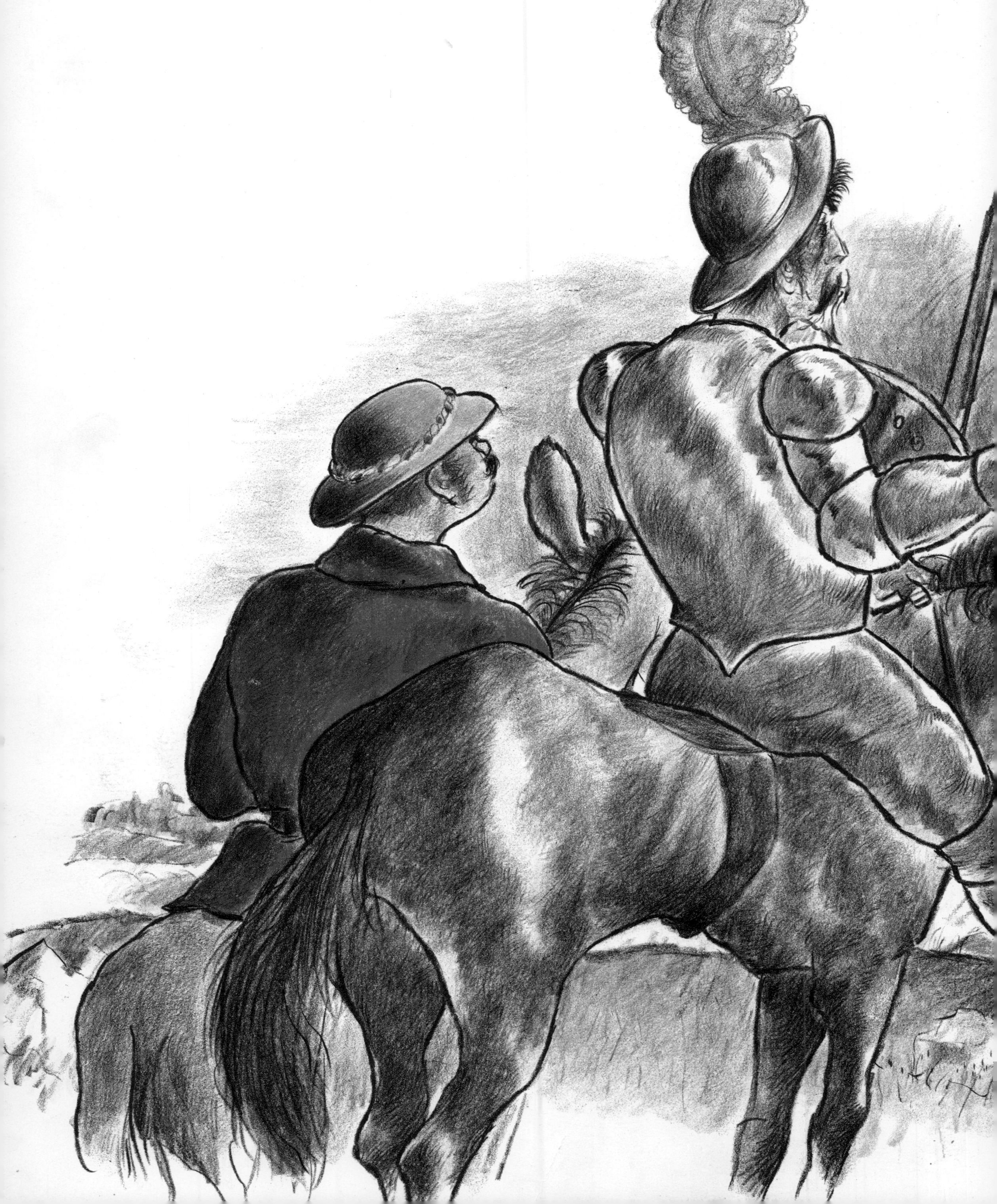

SHEEP AND THE LAMBS

Many days later, when all four could travel again, Don Quixote pointed out a cloud of dust.

"That cloud of dust, Sancho, is raised by an army coming to do battle."

Don points out a cloud of dust...

"In that case, Master Don, there must be two armies for on yonder valley is another cloud of dust," replied Sancho.

"If there are two, we shall aid the weaker one, of course," answered Don.

Don Quixote heard the beating of drums and the sounds of armies.

He heard bugle calls, and the charge of horses.

He heard muskets being fired, and the shouting of soldiers.

He can hear drums...

...and General's horses!

Sancho listened as hard as he could but could hear none of the sounds Don Quixote spoke about.

Don charges them
and gets spilled from his horse

"All I can hear, master, is the bleating of sheep and the mewing of lambs."

But Don Quixote had already charged. What he thought were two armies really turned out to be two flocks of sheep. Rosinante stumbled and once more Don Quixote fell off his horse.

Sancho hurried to aid his stricken master, whose mouth was bleeding. Sancho examined Don Quixote and discovered four teeth were missing.

"You were right," agreed Don. ". . . and even a diamond is not as precious as one's teeth!"

Don did not talk much after that adventure—his mouth hurt.

Sancho discovers Don has lost four teeth

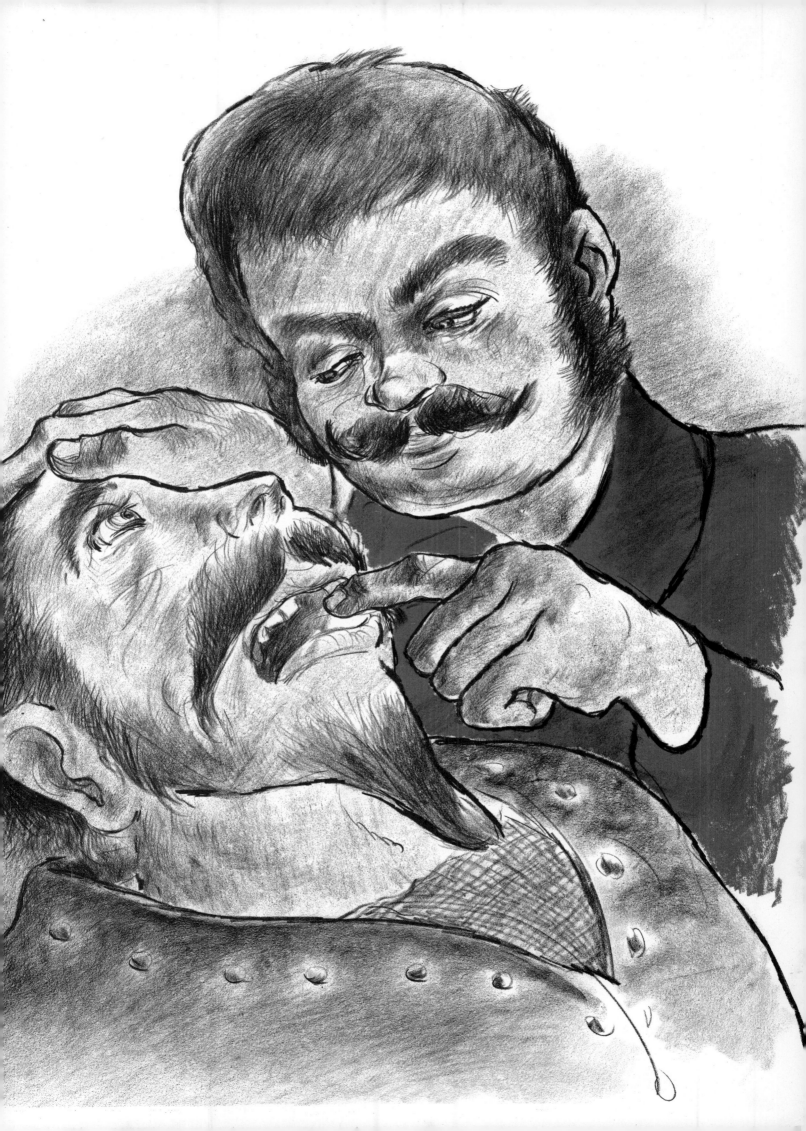

DON QUIXOTE IS KIDNAPED

AFTER months of adventure both Don and Sancho had made many friends. Sometimes they showed their friendship in strange ways. Thus it was that one night while Don was asleep he was kidnaped and carried away in a cage, pajamas, nightcap, and all.

Don is taken in his sleep and carried away

Here's how it happened. . . . Don Quixote had been away for so long and had become so tired that his friends were worried. They tried to convince Don he needed a rest.

When Don refused they made a plan. As soon as Don was fast asleep they would place him in a cage and take him home.

An ox-cart is used to carry the cage

Don didn't like the plan, though he was as comfortable as a knight caged on an oxcart can be. Sancho was unhappy, too, that this fate should befall his friend and master. He was determined to free him somehow. However, the long trip began that very morning. First, there were the oxen, and the

They all began
the long procession...

owner, then Don in a cage on the cart. But right behind followed Sancho on Dapple—and behind *them* Rosinante tagged along. It wasn't long before Sancho caught up with the cart and loosened one of the bars in the

cage. Meanwhile the oxcart kept bumbling along the noisy road. Don Quixote thanked faithful Sancho as he crawled out. Then he quickly mounted Rosinante and they rode off in the opposite direction.

Faithful Sancho follows his friend

SANCHO'S DONKEY IS STOLEN FROM UNDER HIM

THEY rode for hours until the oxcart was far out of sight. Don Quixote, whose sleep had been disturbed anyway, became drowsy

Both adventurers are tired and stop for a nap

and tired. They paused—and Don leaned on his lance and was soon asleep. Sancho fell sound asleep, just as he was.

So soundly did they sleep that Dapple was stolen from under Sancho. He didn't discover it till he awoke. When he opened his eyes and stretched he fell to the ground. Some donkey thieves had replaced Dapple with a log—though not even Don Quixote knew how. Luckily Dapple, in true donkey fashion, refused to budge and waited right there for Sancho to awaken.

Sancho awakes on a wooden horse

THE TRAVELING

CARNIVAL

IT WAS early morning on the high road outside Barcelona when our friends met a traveling company of actors. They were all in a donkey cart: A queen, a bearded lady, a court jester, and others.

One of the clowns
does tricks for Don

At first they thought Don Quixote and
Sancho were actors too, because of the
armor and lance and shield. Then, later,
when they became friends, the court jester,
who was a juggler, performed for Don and
Sancho right there on the road. Rosinante
had never seen a juggler and became skittish.

With one sudden movement he twisted and tossed, and once again Don Quixote fell to the ground.

Rosinante becomes frightened...

...and off comes Don—

The court jester stopped juggling his clubs and helped Don Quixote to his feet.

He was truly sorry to have caused his new-found friend such a fall. With the bells on his cap jingling, he bowed low to Don Quixote and Sancho and apologized.

The clown apologizes
and they all become friends

THE KING'S LIONS

SANCHO will never forget their next adventure, for it happened on his birthday. Coming down the road toward them was a huge wagon driven by two men astride mules. It had gay colored banners flying from the roof.

The lions are carried in a royal wagon

After questions, they soon learned that the wagon contained a wild lion. He was being taken to the King's own menagerie. Don Quixote had never seen a wild or a tame lion, and asked to see him. But the drivers told him the lion was too fierce. Don assured them he was not afraid.

Don takes his first look at a lion

When the wagon was opened Don Quixote
pulled out his sword. To show he was
unafraid he challenged the lion to a duel.
But the lion only yawned.

page 72

The two drivers and Sancho tried to stop
Don Quixote's latest adventure. But the lion

didn't try to stop him. He kept staring at
the sword and the helmet and the armor.
And he kept yawning, much to Don Quixote's
annoyance. Finally the lion saw all there
was to see. After all, though Don Quixote
had never seen a lion, neither had the lion
ever seen a knight in armor.

He soon became drowsy from yawning
and walked to the darkest corner of the

wagon. Curling in a ball like a kitten he fell
fast asleep. The drivers quickly shut the
door and drove off, leaving Don Quixote and
Sancho staring after them.

*...the lion goes
to a corner to sleep*

DON QUIXOTE AND SANCHO TAKE A TRIP TO THE MOON

"THINK of it!" exclaimed Don. "We will be the first to fly to the moon!"

He had agreed to make the trip on a wooden horse that friends had given him. When Sancho asked how a wooden horse was able to fly he was told it was a great secret. Furthermore to keep it a secret, they were to be blindfolded.

"This will be our greatest adventure!" Don was sure.

They are blindfolded and placed atop the magic flying horse

"We are climbing now," said Don Quixote.

*But, he didn't know his friends had pushed a block
under the horse's front feet.*

"Indeed we are," agreed Sancho. "I feel
the wind pushing us from behind."

But, he didn't know another friend was squeezing a bellows.

As they felt the horse turning, Don whispered
to Sancho, "We are returning."
*But they didn't realize two men had turned
the horse around.*

". . . and now the wind blows from the
front!" *But again, neither knew the bellows squeezer had
moved to the front.*

It was all a joke on Don Quixote, for everyone knows wooden horses can't fly. When the block was pulled from under the horse it felt as if they had landed on earth again. But Don Quixote and Sancho were convinced that they had indeed been to the moon. They described the sights they had seen to all who listened and there was no one to challenge them.

They suddenly return to earth

Don is pleased that everyone remembers him

DON QUIXOTE RETURNS HOME

FINALLY there came a day when Don wanted to return home. He wanted to rest, but most of all he wanted to write a book about his adventures. Though he had been gone many years, everyone recognized him and Don Quixote was pleased.

There was a reason for this, though he never did find out. Someone had proclaimed his arrival in an unusual way. For pasted on the back of his armor was a sign which said,

"THIS IS DON QUIXOTE."

...he returns home without knowing why everyone recognized him

PROVERBS OF SANCHO

As much as you have—so much are you worth.

You cannot catch fish without getting wet.

Know yourself; it will keep you from puffing up.

He who is not up with the sun does not enjoy
the day.

He who gives quickly gives twice.

Let every spinster mind her spinning.

Careless dress comes from a careless mind.

Do not ask pears from a maple tree.

The pitcher that goes to the well too often
loses its handle or its spout.

He who has good and chooses evil—let him
not complain.

Don't go looking for five feet on a cat.